For **Joshua,**
the archetypal bold boy
~**M. D.**

For **Dish** and **Keith**
~**J. R.**

First U.S. edition 2001

Library of Congress
Cataloging-in-Publication Data

Doyle, Malachy.
The bold boy / Malachy Doyle ;
illustrated by Jane Ray. — 1st U.S. ed.
p.   cm.
Summary: After his pea is eaten by a hen, the
bold boy tries to exact justice by taking from
their owners a series of increasingly larger animals.
ISBN 0-7636-1624-9
[1. Animals—Fiction.] I. Ray, Jane, ill. II. Title.
PZ7.D775 Bo 2001
[E]—dc21   2001025221

1 2 3 4 5 6 7 8 9 10

Printed in Italy

This book was typeset in FuturaT Bold.
The illustrations were done in watercolor, gouache, pencil, and collage.

Candlewick Press
2067 Massachusetts Avenue
Cambridge, Massachusetts 02140

visit us at www.candlewick.com

THE Bold Boy

Malachy Doyle

illustrated by Jane Ray

CANDLEWICK PRESS
CAMBRIDGE, MASSACHUSETTS

A bold boy

found a pea and he put it
in his nut-brown bag.

Then he did a little dance
and he sang a little song,
and off he toddled.

"**W**ould you watch
this pea for me?"
said the bold boy,
handing it to an
old woman.

He did another little dance,
sang another little song,
and off he toddled.

The woman put
the pea in a bucket,
to keep it safe for
the bold boy.

But a speckled hen
came into the kitchen.
She saw the pea and,
quick as a flash, she ate it.

"I've come for my pea," said the bold boy.

"I'm sorry to say it's been eaten,"
said the old woman.

"By whom?" said the bold boy.

"My speckled hen that's standing there.
She's the one who ate it."

"Naughty, naughty!" cried the bold boy, grabbing ahold of the speckled hen and popping her into his nut-brown bag. "You ate my pea so now you're mine, for that's the law where I come from!"

Then he picked up the bag and off he toddled.

"**W**ill you keep an eye on my hen for me?" said the bold boy, handing her to an old man in the next village.

Then he did a little dance and he sang a little song, and off he toddled.

So the old man made
a pen for the little speckled hen,
and he put her inside.

Pig came to visit
and he frightened Speckled Hen.

She squeaked and squawked,
she flapped her wings,
and over the hill she flew.

"**W**here's my hen?"said the bold boy.

"Frightened away," said the old man.

"**By whom?**" said the bold boy.

"My curious pig,"said the old man.

"**Naughty, naughty!**" cried the bold boy,
popping the pig in his nut-brown bag.
"You're mine, you lump," said he to the pig,
"for that's the law where I come from."

The pig was big, but the boy
was bold and off he
merrily toddled.

"**W**ould you keep an
eye on my pig for me?"
he asked a young girl
in the next village.

The young girl smiled
and said she would.

So he did a little dance
and he sang a little song,
and off he toddled.

The poor old pig was tired,
so he curled up in the stable.
But Donkey didn't want
to have a pig in his bed.
"Hee-haw, hee-haw," he brayed
in the pig's ear.

The sleepy pig was
terrified and scampered
down the lane.

"**W**here's my pig?" said the bold boy.

"Chased away," said the young girl.

"**By whom?**" said the bold boy.

"My lovely donkey," said the young girl.

"**Naughty, naughty!**"
cried the bold boy. "Your donkey's mine now,
for that's the law where I come from."

And up he jumped
and off he galloped.

The donkey was strong
and its legs were long,
but the young girl's
voice was stronger.

"Stop!" she hollered, and
the donkey stopped.

The boy flew off
and up and over,
headfirst into a haystack.

"Naughty!"

The girl came running,
the man came running,
the woman came running,
each of them shouting,

“Naughty!”

“Naughty!”

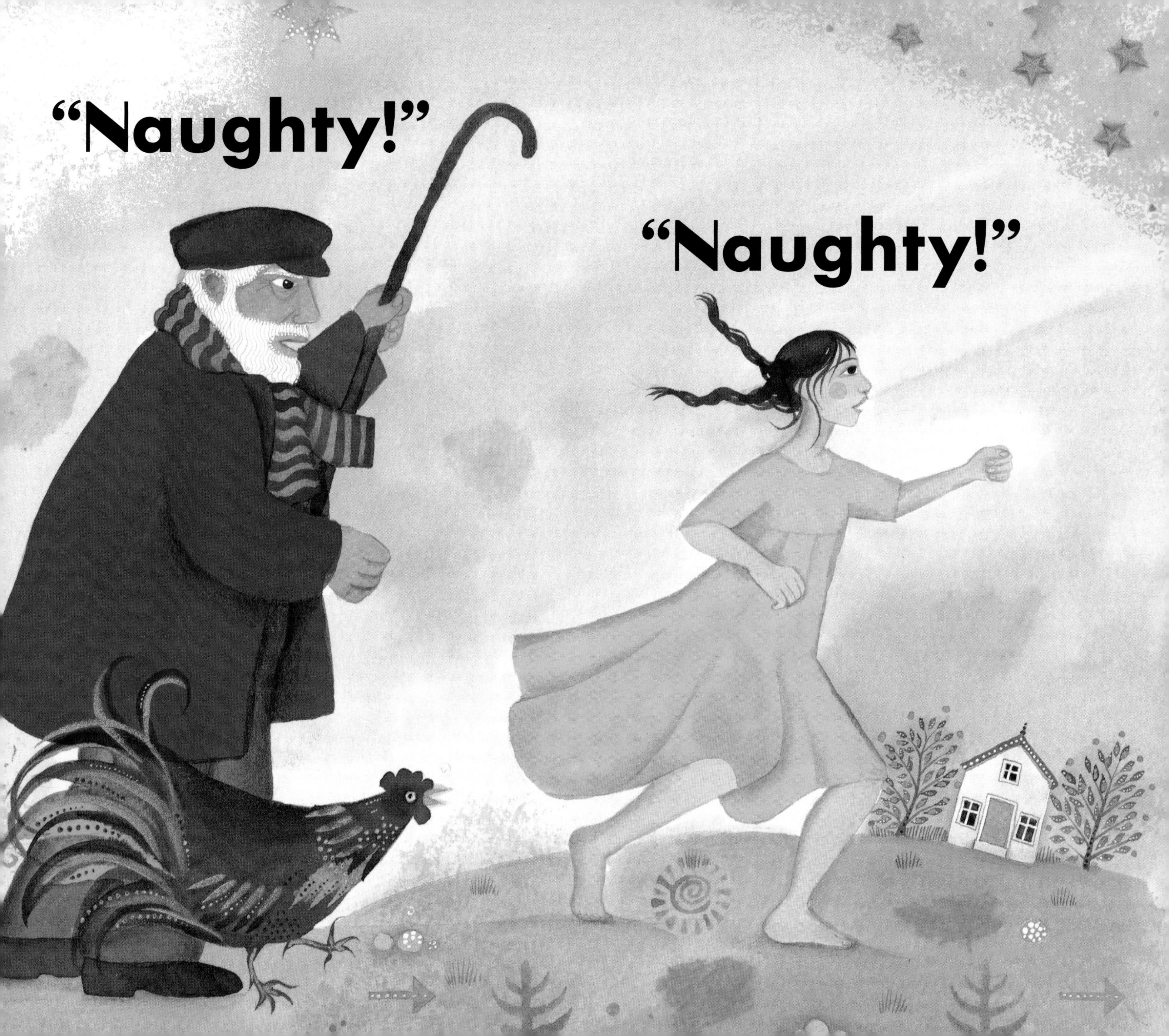

"**Y**ou're the one who's naughty,
stealing a hen and a pig and a donkey.
Make yourself scarce,
you naughty boy, for that's
the law 'round here!"

The bold boy drooped;
he was gloomy; he was glum.
He frowned a mighty frown
and he cast his eyebrows down.

And there,
on the ground,
he spied . . .

a pea!

He whooped
and he scooped
and he popped
it in his bag.

Then he did a little dance
and he sang a little song,
and off he toddled.